SEASONS
OF A RED FOX

SMITHSONIAN
WILD HERITAGE COLLECTION

To Beth Greenfield

SEASONS OF A RED FOX

by Susan Saunders

Illustrated by Jo-Ellen Bosson

Soundprints
PAPERBACKS

A Division of Trudy Management Corporation
Norwalk, Connecticut

Red fox is born in early spring, helpless and blind, in a large den at the edge of a meadow. For four weeks, he and his sister and two brothers live in the den, never venturing aboveground.

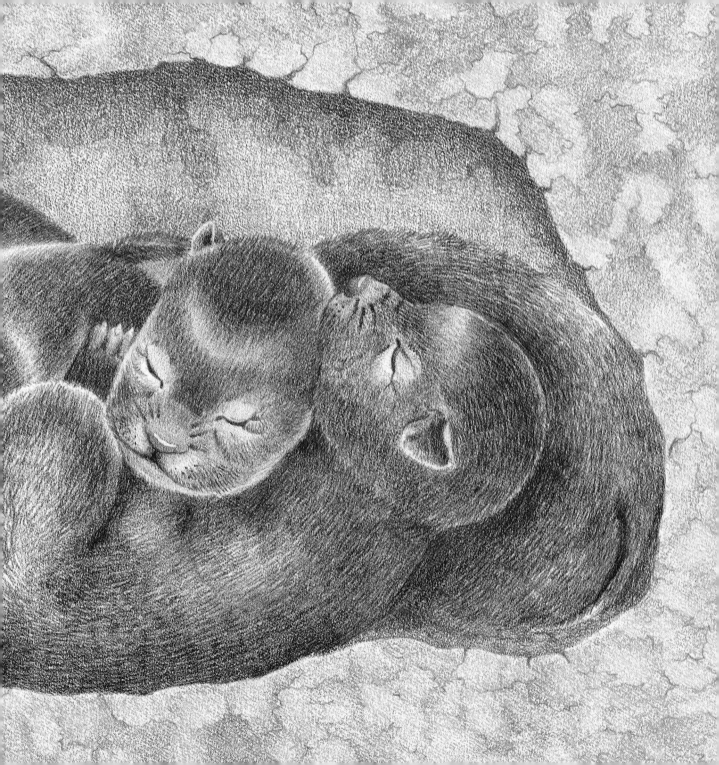

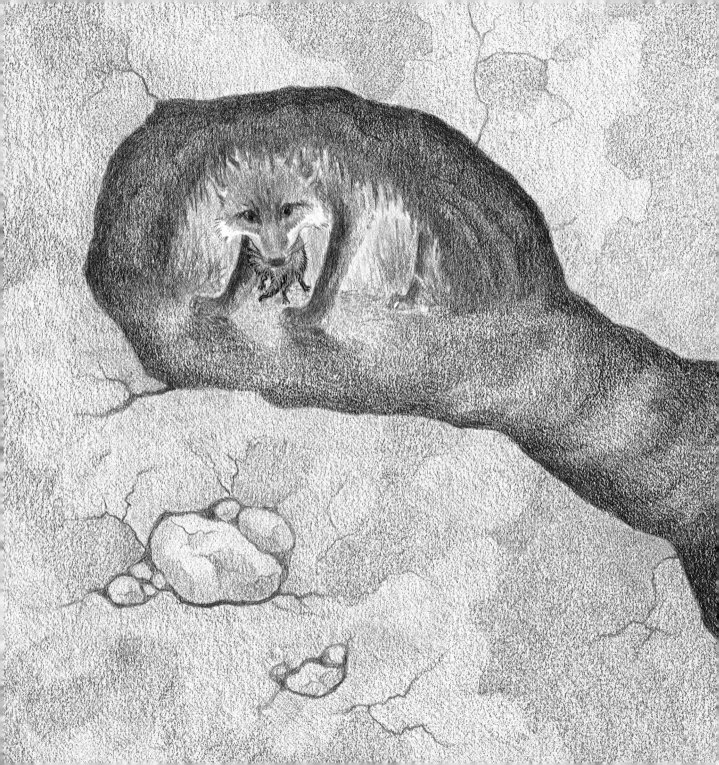

The baby foxes' mother stays in the warm den with them, nursing the kits while her mate hunts. He brings food for her to the entrance of the den: mice and voles, squirrels or birds, sometimes even a fish from a pond not far away.

After a month or so passes, the kits are beginning to eat solid food themselves. Then both parents hunt for the family. The female leaves the den at twilight, but she returns several times during the night to feed her babies.

For Red Fox, spring is a wonderful season. His belly is full, and he plays outside the entrance to the den with his brothers and sister while his mother keeps a careful watch: lively games of chase, and hide-and-seek.

As spring turns into summer, the baby foxes learn to hunt from their mother. She shows Red Fox how to walk silently, without snapping a twig, or even rustling a leaf.

He learns to freeze when he spots the
tiniest movement in the grass, and gathers
himself into a crouch like a cat.

Then he lunges, coming down hard with his front paws in the exact place where the grass has been moving. With luck, he pins his prey to the ground—a lizard, or a plump field mouse.

By midsummer, Red Fox
and his brothers and
sister are almost full-sized.
As their parents bring
them less and less to eat,
the young foxes must
spend more time finding
food on their own, from
grasshoppers to wild blue-
berries, to rabbits.

At summer's end, the young foxes
go their separate ways. Red Fox
makes his own den in a hollow log
on the far side of the pond.

Autumn brings him blackberries
to eat, and wild rose hips. But it also
brings frost, and the first snowfall.

Food grows harder to find, and Red Fox
often goes hungry. He listens for
mice tunneling under the snow.
Once he uncovers the icy leg bone
of a deer, buried by a coyote.

But Red Fox still likes to play. Sometimes
he postpones his nightly hunting trips
to gallop across the frozen pond and slide
and glide in the moonlight.

One night in midwinter, his play is interrupted
by a friendly yelp from the edge of the pond.
Red Fox barks an answer, and a young
female fox trots across the ice to meet him.
Tails wagging, the two foxes touch noses.

Now they will look together for a large den to share, where their own family will be born early in the spring.

About the red fox:

The red fox is born in a burrow or ground den in early spring. The kits remain in the den for a month and begin to roam and actively forage for mice, rabbits, birds, insects, or fruit by 12 weeks of age. Red foxes are found in Eurasia and North America.

Glossary

Den: A hollow or cavern used by a wild animal for protection.

Grasshoppers: Plant-eating insects whose hind legs are adapted for leaping.

Kits: The young of several kinds of mammals, including foxes.

Meadow: Area that is mostly covered by grasses.

Pond: A body of water, usually smaller than a lake.

Predator: An animal that gets its food by catching other animals.

Prey: An animal taken by a predator as food.

Rose hips: Seed pods of roses.

Several: More than two, but fewer than many.

Twilight: A time when the sun has set, but it is not yet full night.

Voles: Small rodents with stout bodies, short legs and tails.

Points of Interest in this Book

pp. 4–7	Red fox kits are born with very dark fur. As they grow, their fur becomes lighter — first around the face and then the entire body, except feet, legs, and ears.
pp. 8–9	By eight weeks, the kits are almost the same color as their parents.
p. 15	Lady slippers.
p. 16	Skink.
p. 19	Grasshopper.
p. 21	Box turtle.
pp. 22–23	Wild rose hips.
p. 25	Cardinal.